原発ガーデン

映画監督デレク・ジャーマンの最晩年

写真

Eden in the shadow of Dungeness
Cinematographer Derek Jarman in his last years

すーべにあ文庫

表紙画／重野克明
英訳／大村じゅん
装丁／宮崎麻代

本書の収益の一部（1冊につき50円）は
「公益財団法人エイズ予防財団」に寄付され、
HIV感染症・エイズに関する正しい知識の
普及啓発等に使用されます。

A part of the proceeds of this book (¥50 per copy) will be donated to Japan Foundation for AIDS Protection. It is used for raising public awareness and conveying accurate information about HIV infection and AIDS.

Derek Jarman

デレク・ジャーマン

1942〜1994

映画監督
　　舞台美術家
　　　　詩人

　　　　　　　園芸家

The film director, set designer, poet and gardener.

1986年
HIVに罹ったことをきっかけに
ダンジネスに住む。

In 1986, Jarman was diagnosed as HIV positive.
His illness prompted him to move to Prospect Cottage,
Dungeness.

そこは何もないところです。

In the middle of nowhere.

風をさえぎるところが何もない、
地の果てを
連想させるような場所。

原発が建設されたために、
漁師たちから捨てられた場所。

In this desolate landscape, the silence is only broken by
the wind. Nuclear power stations were built, the fisher-
man's sheds were left abandoned.

The sky pierced and torn no longer sheltered the naked earth.(The Garden)

天は裂かれ　もはや　大地はむきだしに
映画「ザ・ガーデン」より

ダンジネスの原発は2基。
1基はすでに止まっているが、
停止した原発が廃炉になるのは、
100年後。

Two Dungeness nuclear power plants – A and B.
Dungeness B is to stay open. Dungeness A ceased, but
it will take 100 years to decommission.

For million years thirty thousand unborn generations bound to the memory of criminal rulers.(The Garden)

未来の三万世代は　百万年
罪深い統治者たちの名声に　苦しむことになる
映画「ザ・ガーデン」より

彼はその地に庭をつくった。

He created his own garden in the wilderness.

彼のガーデニングは、
草花だけでなく、漂流してきた木や
腐った鉄などを使っていた。

He began to build an unusual garden – glowing plants, collecting stones, rusting metal and driftwood from the beach.

Remember, to be going and to have are not eternal.
(The Garden)

覚えておくがいい 存在とは 永久ではないということを
映画「ザ・ガーデン」より

「死に向かっている物」を集めて、
ここに楽園をつくろうとした。

Filling with his collections – approaching the end of life
– from the shoreline. Eden: feeling at peace.

私がはじめて
彼の家（プロスペクトコテージ）を訪れたのは、
1989年夏のこと。

In summer 1989, I paid my first visit to his 'Prospect Cottage'.

「写真、いい？」と私が聞くと、
「いいよ」と彼が答える。

(showing my camera) "Can I ... ?" I ask.
"Sure!" he nods with a smile.

If the doors of Perception were cleansed then everything would be seen as it is.(BLUE)
もし知覚の扉が清らかだったなら　すべてがあるがままに見えるのだろう
映画「ブルー」より

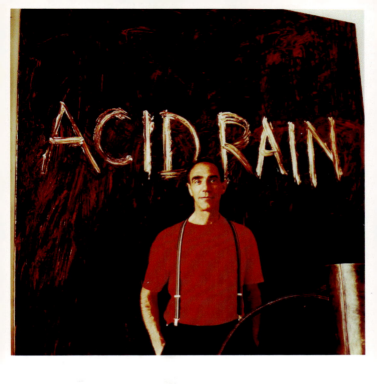

すーべにあ文庫『原発ガーデン　映画監督デレク・ジャーマンの最晩年』
写真と文／奥宮誠次

POST CARD

ダンジネスは、
天候次第で大きく印象が変わる。
同じように、彼の体調も変化しているように
思えた。

Dungeness changes its appearance depending upon the
weather, and his health condition also varies.

What if the present were the world's last night?
(The Garden)

もしも　今夜　世界が終わってしまったなら？
映画「ザ・ガーデン」より

ゲイというマイノリティで、
HIVという人生。
彼はダンジネスと自分を重ねあわせるところ
があったのではないだろうか。

His fights for gay rights and HIV awareness, this is a
place where Dungeness and himself overlap.

彼はこの地に、庭をつくった。
完成することのない、最後の作品。

He created an extraordinary garden amid the harsh landscape – his last great artwork unfinished.

It was the last photoshoot of Derek Jarman one-and-a-half years before his death.
The day he wasn't well, but in spite of this he kindly invited me to dinner.

"Let's have a smile," he said with a big smile as he braced himself.

"See you!" I said, but I didn't think it would be goodbye forever.

わたしが最後にデレクの写真を撮ったのは、
彼が亡くなる1年半ほど前。
体調はいつにもまして悪そうだったが、
彼は気を使って食事に誘ってくれた。

Let's have a smile.
自分を奮い立たせるように、そう言って笑顔
をつくった。

See you.
それがデレクと会う最後になるとは思わず、
私たちはごく自然に別れた。

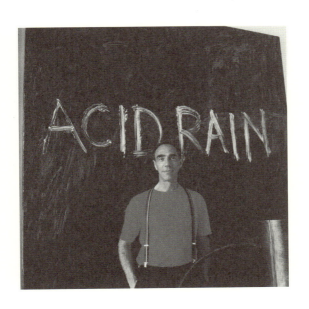

さよなら、ジェントルマン

私がデレク・ジャーマンを知ったのは1987年、渋谷のシネマライズで上映していた「カラヴァッジオ」を観たことがきっかけだった。1986年に私は住まいをロンドンに移したが、その翌年に休暇で東京に帰ったときに、映画を観に行ったのである。当時としては珍しいゲイ、宗教的なものをモチーフとした作品で分かりづらいけれども、私は写真家という仕事柄、美しい映像がとても印象に残った。

移住して3年が過ぎた頃、知人がデレク・ジャーマンに会いに行くというので、私も連れていってほしいと頼んだ。デレクの名前を聞いた瞬間、「カラヴァッジオ」のシーンが脳裏によみがえったのだ。

こうして、私は初めてダンジネスにデレクを訪ねることとなった。当時の私の下手な英語にもかかわらず、いかにも英国のジェントルマン然としたデレクは親切で、気さくに笑顔を向けてくれた。

デレクと私は少し不思議な関係だった。私は撮影のためにデレクを訪ねたが、別段仕事でもないし、かといって友人でもないので、会うための約束はしなかった。

たとえば、ある朝、私は自宅があったノッティングヒルから、ミニクラブマンの滑らかなエンジンの音を響かせて、ダンジネス

へと向かう。ダンジネスまで車で1時間半。到着するとドアをノックし、カメラを見せて挨拶をする。
そして、彼は黙々と自分の作業を続けて、私は控えめにシャッターを切る。長いときは1日中、撮影をした。

初めて会ってから4年の間に、私がプロスペクトコテージに行ったのは5回ほどである(仕事では、平凡社から出ていた雑誌「太陽」の撮影が一度だけあった)。
日記帳を確認すると、私が最後にダンジネスを訪ねたのは92年の8月で、彼が亡くなる1年半ほど前であった。
晩年のデレクは、新聞社の取材をよく受けていて、彼の写真が新聞(インディペンデント紙やガーディアン紙)に載るたびに、痩せて、元気がなくなっていくように見えた。

デレクの死後1年ほどたった頃、バービカン・センターというロンドンにある大きな芸術劇場で、彼の回顧展開催の計画が持ち上がった。
デレクのポートレートを飾っていた私の個展を見たバービカンの学芸員から、写真を出展してほしいという依頼があった。
それで、ネガ、ポジ、紙焼き、自分の持っているほとんどすべてのデレクの写真をバービカン側に貸与すると、回顧展の準備中にそれらすべてを紛失してしまった。
不運にも写真は失われた。しかしそのことよりも、彼の回顧

展に協力できないことのほうが私は残念だった。
いつかどこかで、それらが表に出てくることを願っている。
現在、私が所有しているデレクの写真は20枚ほどで、そのほとんどが本書に収められている。
わずかに手元に残った彼の写真である。

奇しくも福島の原発事故があった翌2012年、四半世紀ぶりに私は日本で暮らすようになった。
デレクが亡くなって20年以上もたってから、こうして彼の写真を収めた小さな本が完成した。22年前の回顧展には出展できなかったけれども、何となく肩の荷が下りたような——これでようやく、彼と本当のお別れができるような気がする。

　　　　　　　　　　　　　　　2018年5月　奥宮誠次

Saying Goodbye to a Gentleman

I got to know Derek Jarman in 1987 when I saw his film 'Caravaggio' at Cinema Rise in Shibuya.

I moved to London in 1986. The following year, I was on holiday in Tokyo and went to the cinema in Shibuya.

In those days, it was uncommon to see a film based on gay motif or religious imagery – not easy to understand. However, as a photographer, I was absolutely fascinated by the artistic visual images.

Three years later, my acquaintance said that he was visiting Derek. I asked him whether I could come with him – recalling the film 'Caravaggio'.
Then, I had a chance to pay my first visit to Derek in Dungeness (1989). Despite my broken English at that time, Derek greeted me gentlemanly and warmly with his gentle smile.

Looking back at our relationship, it was really unique.
Although I visited Derek for photographing, as I had no apparent reason – neither for business nor our friendship – I didn't make contact with him before visiting. I had lived in Notting Hill at that time.
I remember one morning, for instance, my MINI Clubman purred along the road – heading towards Dover. It took me an hour and a half to Dungeness. Having arrived there, I knocked on the door gently and gave a signal – showing him my camera. Then, he continued his work silently, and I started to take photographs quietly. Sometimes I spent the whole day there.

For four years from 1989, I personally visited 'Prospect Cottage' about five times (visited on business only once for a monthly magazine, 'Taiyo' (Heibonsha)).
Looking at my old diary, it was in August 1992 – one-and-a-half years

before his death – I last visited Dungeness.

In his late years, he was interviewed by the press, such as the Independent, the Guardian and so on. Every time I saw him in the paper, he looked thinner and less energetic.

About one year after the death of Derek, the Barbican Centre, London (Europe's largest arts centre) was planning to hold his Exhibition.
    "Derek Jarman: A Retrospective" (1996)
Their curator asked me whether I could lend them my photographs of Derek Jarman for the exhibition. He had seen Derek's portrait on display at my exhibition before. I lent them most of my photographs of him – negatives, positives and prints.
However, what happened was that they lost all the photos during preparation. Unfortunately I lost my photos, but at that time I was more disappointed not to cooperate with the Retrospective. I am now hoping to see my missing photos somewhere someday.
Only about 20 photos left in my hand – mostly appearing in this book.

In 2012 – a year after the Fukushima Nuclear Power Plant Accident – I moved back to Tokyo after 26 years in London.
It's been more than 20 years since the death of Derek Jarman.
I was sorry I wasn't able to take part in the retrospective exhibition 22 years ago. Now, I feel relieved with this publication.
Today, I pay tribute to Derek Jarman – saying thank you and goodbye to a true legend and gentleman.

Seiji Okumiya
May 2018

ダンジネス原子力発電所

ロンドンから直線距離で約20キロ、ダンジネス岬に現存する原子力発電所。同じ敷地内に建設時期の異なる2つの施設がある。ダンジネスBの2基はトラブル続きで断続的に運転を停止。ダンジネスAは2009年までに燃料取り出しを完了したが、最終的な廃炉は2111年を予定している。

デレク・ジャーマン

1942年生まれのイギリスの映画監督。舞台デザイナー、作家としての顔も持ち、特に日本では園芸家として有名。「イン・ザ・シャドウ・オブ・ザ・サン」(1974年) で映画監督デビュー。生前よりゲイであることを公表し、1986年にHIVへの感染が判明。1994年、死去。主な映画監督作品に「カラヴァッジオ」「ガーデン」「ウィトゲンシュタイン」、遺作となった「ブルー」がある。

奥宮誠次 (おくみや・せいじ)

高知県生まれ。写真家。1986年に渡英し、ロンドンを拠点に主にヨーロッパで活動。2012年、再び東京に活動の拠点を移す。「Anchovy Studio」設立。主な著書に『世界の動物園』『風が笑えば』(俵万智との共著) などがある。

Dungeness Nuclear Power Station
The distance from London to Dungeness is about 20 km in a straight line.
Two nuclear power plants – Dungeness A and Dungeness B – are located on the Dungeness headland in the south of Kent, England. The construction of the two plants was carried out at different times.
Due to many problems with two units at Dungeness B, intermittent shutdowns continued. Dungeness A ceased, and defuelling was completed by 2009, with final decommissioning scheduled for 2111.

Derek Jarman
Derek Jarman (1942–1994) was an English film director, set designer, author, especially known as a gardener in Japan.
His debut film is In the Shadow of the Sun (1974). Following his public announcement that he was gay, he was diagnosed as HIV positive in 1986.
Derek Jarman created extraordinary feature films – including Caravaggio, The Garden, Wittgenstein, and Blue (his last film).

Seiji Okumiya
Photographer. He was born in Kochi. He moved to London in 1986, photographing mostly in Europe. In 2012 he moved back to Tokyo and established 'Anchovy Studio'. Publications: PLANET ZOO, Kazega waraeba (with Machi Tawara) etc.

すーべにあ文庫について

情報が氾濫する時代、「大切なことは、きっと紙に書いてある」をスローガンにすーべにあ文庫（souvenir＝贈り物、の意）は創刊されました。文庫の収益は、各テーマに関連する団体・施設に寄付されます。大切なことが、大切にしたい誰かに伝わりますように。あなたの読む、知る、考えるが社会貢献につながります。

すーべにあ文庫04

原発ガーデン　映画監督デレク・ジャーマンの最晩年

2018年9月30日　発行

著者　奥宮誠次

発行　株式会社百年書房
　　　〒130-0021 東京都墨田区緑1-13-2 山崎ビル201
　　　TEL:03-6666-9594　　HP:100shobo.com

本書のコピー、スキャン、デジタル化等の無断複製を禁じます。
Ⓒ Seiji Okumiya 2018 Printed in Japan
ISBN978-4-907081-44-7　C0136